DC SUPER HERO
FAIRY TALES

SUPERGIRL™
AND THE CINDER GAMES

BY LAURIE S. SUTTON
ILLUSTRATED BY AGNES GARBOWSKA
COLORS BY SIL BRYS

SUPERGIRL BASED ON CHARACTERS CREATED
BY JERRY SIEGEL AND JOE SHUSTER BY SPECIAL
ARRANGEMENT WITH THE JERRY SIEGEL FAMILY

Published by Stone Arch Books, an imprint of Capstone
1710 Roe Crest Drive, North Mankato, Minnesota 56003
capstonepub.com

Library of Congress Cataloging-in-Publication Data
Names: Sutton, Laurie, author. | Garbowska, Agnes, illustrator.
Title: Supergirl and the Cinder Games / by Laurie S. Sutton ; illustrated
by Agnes Garbowska.
Description: North Mankato, Minnesota : Stone Arch Books, an imprint
of Capstone, [2021] | Series: DC super hero fairy tales | Audience: Ages
8-11. | Audience: Grades 4-6. | Summary: A prisoner on the planet
Apokolips, her memory of her powers suppressed, Supergirl has been
reduced to a serving girl for Granny Goodness and the Female Furies;
but when she watches trainees prepare for the Cinder Games something
in their moves is familiar, and with the help of a Mother Box she enters
the games in disguise and wins, recovers her true identity, and escapes
through a portal, leaving only a boot behind.
Identifiers: LCCN 2021016019 (print) | LCCN 2021016020 (ebook) | ISBN
9781663910592 (hardcover) | ISBN 9781663921406 (paperback) | ISBN
9781663910561 (pdf)
Subjects: LCSH: Supergirl (Fictitious character)—Juvenile fiction. |
Superheroes—Juvenile fiction. | Supervillains—Juvenile fiction. |
Memory—Juvenile fiction. | Identity (Psychology)—Juvenile fiction. |
Fairy tales—Adaptations. | CYAC: Fairy tales. | Superheroes—Fiction. |
Supervillains—Fiction. | Memory—Fiction. | identity—Fiction. | LCGFT:
Fairy tales. | Superhero fiction.
Classification: LCC PZ8.S92 Su 2021 (print) | LCC PZ8.S92 (ebook) |
DDC 813.54 [Fic]—dc23
LC record available at https://lccn.loc.gov/2021016019
LC ebook record available at https://lccn.loc.gov/2021016020

Designed by Hilary Wacholz

TABLE OF CONTENTS

ONCE UPON A TIME . . .

THE WORLD'S GREATEST
SUPER HEROES COLLIDED WITH
THE WORLD'S BEST-KNOWN
FAIRY TALES TO CREATE . . .

DC SUPER HERO
FAIRY TALES

Now, Supergirl is secretly entering the Cinder Games of Apokolips, a grand test of skill. She must beat the competition before her shining armor falls to pieces. But can she escape the hold of the wicked Granny Goodness in this twisted retelling of "Cinderella"?

CHAPTER 1

FROM SUPERGIRL TO SERVANT GIRL

ZOOOOM!

Supergirl flew over the blue ocean at super-speed. She had heard an SOS coming from a cargo ship somewhere on the water. Now she was racing to the rescue. She used her telescopic vision to search for it. When Supergirl finally spotted the ship, she was surprised by what she saw.

A swarm of flying humanlike creatures buzzed around the ship!

Each one had a set of mechanical wings. Helmets covered their heads. Green uniforms with golden armor protected their bodies.

Parademons! Supergirl realized. *They're the attack soldiers of Darkseid. He's the evil ruler of the planet Apokolips. It's basically a war world. Has he come to conquer Earth?*

The Girl of Steel sped up and arrived at the cargo ship in seconds. She rammed into a group of the creatures.

KAAPOOOW!

The hit tossed some Parademons into the water. Others were thrown high into the sky.

I don't see Darkseid, Supergirl thought. *But the Parademons didn't come here by themselves. Who is commanding them?*

Suddenly a figure took off from the deck of the ship and flew toward Supergirl.

It was a short, round woman with gray hair. She also wore a green uniform and gripped a short rod in one hand. The rod crackled with energy.

"Granny Goodness, the leader of the Female Furies of Apokolips!" Supergirl said. "What are you doing here?"

Granny did not answer. Instead, she fired a powerful bolt of energy from her mega-rod.

ZZAAAAT!

"AAAHHHH!" Supergirl yelled as the bolt hit her. She wobbled in midair.

ZZAAAT! ZZAAAT!

Two more blasts struck the Girl of Steel. This time she was knocked out. Parademons caught her before she fell into the water. They held her as Granny Goodness put a high-tech band over the Super Hero's head.

"You fell into my trap, Kryptonian," Granny said to the sleeping Supergirl. "This headband will make you forget who you are. You will forget your power of flight, so you cannot flee. But I will allow you to keep some powers so that you may better serve me on Apokolips."

Granny Goodness took a Mother Box from her belt. The device looked like a small box, but it had many amazing abilities. Granny used it to open a portal through space called a Boom Tube.

BOOOOM!

The Parademons carried Supergirl into the portal. Granny Goodness followed them. Their destination—Apokolips!

Supergirl woke to the sound of someone yelling.

"Girl! Girl!"

It took a while for Supergirl to realize that the person was yelling at her.

Why are they calling me "girl"? Supergirl wondered. *My name is . . . I can't remember.*

Supergirl got up from her sleeping spot at the edge of a giant firepit. The pit was set in the stone floor of a huge dining hall and had burned down to cinders. The tattered apron Supergirl wore was covered in ashes.

The only clean thing on her was the metal headband. Supergirl did not realize that she had the strength to remove it. The band kept her from even thinking to try.

"Girl!" a large woman roared, stomping into the room. "Where is my breakfast?"

This was Stompa. She was one of the Female Furies, a group of elite warriors trained by Granny Goodness. She had arms and legs as big as tree trunks.

WHUMP!

Stompa sat down at one of the tables.

Before Supergirl could react, another woman came into the dining hall. She was tall and thin. She snapped a metal whip toward Supergirl.

SKRAAAK!

This was Lashina, another Female Fury.

"Girl! Why isn't my armor polished?" Lashina said. She tossed a body harness at Supergirl.

"Sorry!" Supergirl replied. She caught the harness and zoomed away at super-speed.

"Hurry up! Don't keep us waiting!" Stompa yelled.

ZOOOM! SWOOOSH!

Supergirl returned in a few seconds. She was carrying a tray of food for the Furies in one hand and Lashina's polished armor in the other.

"You missed a spot!" Lashina said without even looking at her armor.

ZOOOM! SWOOOSH!

Supergirl left and returned with the armor in a blur of motion. Lashina took it from Supergirl and dropped it on the floor.

"Girl!" Granny Goodness shouted as she entered the dining hall. "The trainees are coming. Go make breakfast for them!"

"Yes, Granny! Right away!" Supergirl said.

As the Girl of Steel sped away, Stompa and Lashina laughed.

"Ha, ha, ha! She's so eager to please us!" Stompa said. "She'll do anything we say."

Granny sat down at the table next to her Female Furies. Her lips stretched into a wicked smile.

"I see you are enjoying our new servant girl," Granny said. "It also gives me great pleasure to see the high-and-mighty Kryptonian hero brought down to the lowest level."

"And that headband will continue to keep her in check," Lashina added.

Even though Supergirl had super-hearing, she did not hear Granny Goodness and the Female Furies talking about her. She was too busy in the kitchen making breakfast.

Supergirl used her heat vision to heat up giant kettles on the stoves. She zipped around at super-speed gathering ingredients. There was no recipe. Supergirl grabbed whatever was nearby and put it into the pots.

The kettles quickly came to a boil. Supergirl dished out the food into bowls and piled them on to a giant tray. She then used her super-strength to lift the tray and take the bowls into the dining hall. When she arrived, the trainees were just starting to sit at the tables.

None of them smiled, and no one spoke. Supergirl could see why. Granny Goodness stood at one end of the room and glared. She tapped her mega-rod in one hand, as if eager for a reason to use it.

"Hurry up! Eat!" Granny ordered. "The last one out on the training field will suffer!"

The trainees gobbled up as much food as they could. Then they leaped to their feet and rushed away. It did not matter if they were finished. Lashina, Stompa, and Granny followed them out of the dining hall.

"Girl! Clean up this mess!" Granny Goodness ordered as she left.

Supergirl gathered the half-empty bowls at super-speed. She took them outside to the washing vat. As she worked, she could see the trainees practicing their hand-to-hand combat skills. Something about their motions seemed familiar. Somewhere deep inside, Supergirl felt like she had done that before.

ZAP!

Suddenly the metal band around Supergirl's head sent out a sharp spark. The thought was quickly forgotten.

CHAPTER 2

High Hopes

Supergirl sat next to a raging firepit in the armory as she polished a huge stack of armor. The heat from the flames was intense, but she did not feel it. Her Kryptonian body could not be harmed by heat or cold—even if she did not remember that fact.

The task was boring, and she let her focus wander. That's when her super-hearing picked up Lashina and Stompa talking in another room.

"Darkseid has declared that the Cinder Games are to be held in three days!" Lashina said.

"I cannot wait to stomp on the competition!" Stompa replied.

"Ha! I cannot wait to win the prize!" Lashina boasted.

"You're going to need more than that whip of yours to beat me," Stompa said.

"I'll beat you and every other contestant," Lashina said.

"There will be a lot of them! The Games are open to all the warriors on Apokolips," Stompa said.

"I have the speed, strength, and skill to win," Lashina said.

"So do I!" Stompa replied.

There's going to be a special competition? Supergirl thought. *I have speed, strength, and other abilities. I could enter the contest and prove that my skills can be used for something more important than just cooking and cleaning.*

"I need special armor," Stompa said. "I want to look my best when I come in first."

"Me too!" Lashina replied.

Supergirl heard a scuffle. Soon, the Furies were at the door of the armory, elbowing each other to be first inside. Supergirl kept her head down. She hoped that they would ignore her. It was a hope denied.

"Girl! Give me that helmet!" Stompa said as she snatched the piece of armor Supergirl was polishing. The woman shoved the helmet on her head but tossed it away a moment later. "Ugh, it's too tight."

"Ha! That's because you have such a big head!" Lashina said as she grabbed a pair of gloves from the pile. She pulled them over her hands but tugged them off. "Ugh, they're too big."

The two Female Furies went through the entire armory, looking for the perfect gear. Supergirl dashed at super-speed to fetch armguards and helms, visors and gloves, boots and belts.

ZOOM! SWOOSH! ZOOM! SWOOSH!

At last, Stompa and Lashina had armor that pleased each of them. They strutted out of the room with their chosen pieces. The rest of the armor was left in messy piles all over the floor.

"Girl! Straighten up that mess!" Stompa called as she and Lashina left.

Supergirl heard the two Furies laughing down the hallway, but she did not care. Her imagination was churning. The feelings she had when she watched the trainees came back to her.

She reached for a helmet.

ZAP!

The metal band around her head sent out a sharp spark.

But Supergirl was determined. *No. I'm going to do this,* she decided.

She reached for the helmet again. The spark was not as strong. Supergirl smiled and picked up the battle helmet.

This feels good, Supergirl thought as she put it on her head. She put on a glove next. *No, this is too loose.* She found another pair that fit better.

Supergirl tried on boots and shoulder plates and shin guards. When she was finished, she used her heat vision and freeze breath to soften, mold, and then harden the armor to fit her exactly.

Stompa and Lashina can't do that, Supergirl thought.

Supergirl pretended to battle an opponent to test the fit of the armor. She dodged imaginary blows. She kicked with her feet and jabbed with her fists. The motions came naturally to her, as if she already knew them.

This armor will work! Supergirl thought. *I'll be ready for the Cinder Games!*

Supergirl smiled for the first time in as long as she could remember. She hid her special armor in an old trunk. Then she began the task of putting away all the jumbled armor.

At last, the day of the Cinder Games arrived. It was the only thing that anyone on Apokolips could talk about. The contest did not happen very often. It was only held whenever Darkseid commanded. The Games were meant to find the best warrior on the planet. That warrior would become one of Darkseid's personal guards.

Supergirl was excited too. She could not wait to put on her armor and go to the Games. But first she had to help Stompa and Lashina put on their armor.

"Girl! Fix this chinstrap! Stompa broke it!" Lashina yelled.

"I did not! You picked a crummy helmet," Stompa replied.

Supergirl used her heat vision to melt the metal strap back onto the helmet.

"I wonder what sort of obstacle course Darkseid created for the Cinder Games this time," Lashina said as she fussed with her gloves. "Girl! My gloves are loose!"

Supergirl used her super-strength to squeeze the metal gloves tighter around Lashina's wrists.

"It will be harder than the last one, I'm sure," Stompa replied as she shoved her feet into a pair of metal boots. "Ugh! These boots are too tight! Girl!"

Supergirl rushed over to Stompa. She dug her fingers into the sides of the boots and stretched them out. Stompa tested the fit with a super-stomp of both feet.

BWOOOM! BWOOOM!

The whole room shook and rattled as if an earthquake had hit. Rat creatures scurried out of the walls and fled for somewhere safer.

"Nice fit," Stompa said. "I am ready. See you at the finish line, Lashina!"

"Not if I get there first!" Lashina replied as they left the room.

Supergirl waited for the Female Furies to be out of sight. Then she zoomed to the armory to put on her special armor. A few seconds later, she raced to catch up to Granny Goodness and the Furies as they left the training center.

"Granny, I want to go to the Cinder Games!" Supergirl said. "Look, I made my own armor!"

"Don't be ridiculous. You're a servant girl, not a warrior!" Granny said angrily.

The villain knew that if Darkseid found out she had the Kryptonian Super Hero, he would be furious. She would be punished for keeping it a secret.

Granny ripped off a part of Supergirl's armor. "This is from the armory. It doesn't belong to you!"

"This is from the armory too!" Stompa said. She pulled the helmet off Supergirl's head and crushed it under her foot.

"And this! And this!" Lashina said.

The Female Furies tore apart Supergirl's armor. The pieces landed in a heap around her feet. The villains laughed as they left the training center.

"Clean up this mess, girl," Granny Goodness ordered. Then she followed the Furies out the door.

CHAPTER 3

A Little Help from a Friend

Supergirl slowly picked up the ruined armor from the ground. She did not move at super-speed. She dragged her feet as she walked through the empty training center. No one was there. They had all gone to the Cinder Games.

Supergirl carried the metal pieces to the trash dump outside of the training center. The place smelled terrible, but Supergirl was so unhappy that she hardly noticed.

Rat creatures dug through the piles of rotting kitchen waste and other junk. Supergirl dropped the ruined armor near one of the heaps. Then she sat down on top of the armor and started to cry.

"It's not fair. All I wanted was to go to the Cinder Games," Supergirl sobbed.

A rat creature paused nearby. It sat up on its hind feet as if listening to Supergirl.

"I have the speed and the strength to compete. I use them all the time!" Supergirl told the animal. "And I have other skills that none of the trainees have. Not even Stompa or Lashina."

SIZZZZ!

Supergirl used her heat vision to set part of the trash heap on fire.

"None of them can do that!" Supergirl said.

The rat creature squeaked in alarm and scampered to safety. Supergirl sighed and put out the blaze with a puff of her super-breath.

"They can't do that, either," Supergirl muttered. "I have all these powers. I should be using them to . . . help people."

A moment later, Supergirl noticed that the trash fire had exposed a small metal box. The box was twisted and bent, but there was not a single burn mark on it.

That thing looks familiar, Supergirl thought as she reached for the box.

ZAP!

A spark flared from the headband. Supergirl shook off the sting and picked up the box. As soon as she touched it, the device made a clear sound.

PING!

A wave of gratitude washed over Supergirl. Somehow, she knew the feeling was coming from the box. It was saying thanks.

"Oh! You're welcome," Supergirl replied. She turned the object over in her hands. Little did she know, it was a Mother Box. It was a living piece of Apokolips technology. "You're in pretty bad shape. Let me try to fix that."

Supergirl focused her heat vision on the device to reshape it as she had done with the armor. It did not work.

This box is made from something completely different than the armor, Supergirl realized. *I don't know that I can fix it.*

PING!

A thought whispered through her mind that she had more power than she knew.

"Okay! Let's try this again!" Supergirl said.

Twin beams of ultrahot energy shot out from Supergirl's eyes. They struck the Mother Box in her hands and surrounded it in a fiery glow. Supergirl did not feel the incredible heat, but she could feel the metal starting to soften. It did not take her long to smooth out the walls of the twisted box.

"Is that better?" Supergirl asked the box.

PING!

A wave of happiness washed over her.

"I'm glad I could help," Supergirl said. "I wish you could help *me*."

PING?

"I wanted to go to the Cinder Games, but Stompa and Lashina ruined my armor," Supergirl said. "All I wanted was a chance."

PING!

The Mother Box began to glow. The glow grew until it covered Supergirl and the armor she was sitting on. Suddenly the armor started to shake. Supergirl jumped to her feet.

"Are you doing that?" Supergirl gasped.

PING!

The bits of wrecked armor rose up into the air. The glow became a ball of sparkling light. Supergirl watched in awe as the pieces of armor were transformed. Dented bits of metal became beautiful boots and gloves and armguards. The helmet that Stompa had squashed became a fabulous battle helm.

At last, the sparkling light began to fade. The armor floated through the air and settled onto Supergirl's body.

"It's a perfect fit!" Supergirl exclaimed.

Then she realized another problem.
"But . . . I will never make it to the Cinder Games before the contest starts."

PING!

The device was not finished. Metal pieces started to rise up out of the trash piles from all over the dump. Some pieces were small, and some were large. Rat creatures jumped out of the way of a metal chunk the size of a big pumpkin.

The scraps of junk came together like pieces of a jigsaw puzzle. Supergirl watched in amazement as the rusty metal mess turned into the most beautiful car she had ever seen.

"This is incredible," Supergirl said. "Thank you!"

PING!

A wave of encouragement washed over Supergirl as she hugged the little Mother Box.

"Let's do this!" Supergirl declared. She tucked the Mother Box into her belt and then jumped into the car.

VROOOOM!

The car powered up its antigravity engine and sped away from the training center. It seemed to know where it was going. It zoomed through the crowded sky-streets. All the traffic was heading toward the Cinder Games.

In the distance, Supergirl could see the huge stadium where the Games were being held. It was an enormous oval bowl that looked as if it had been carved out of a single block of stone. Gigantic flaming torches were set all around the top.

Hundreds of flying cars were coming in for a landing, but they all gave way to Supergirl's incredible vehicle. People whispered in awe when they saw her step out of the car.

"Who is that?"

"Such amazing armor!"

"She must be an important warrior!"

Suddenly Supergirl saw Granny Goodness, Lashina, and Stompa a few steps ahead of her. They turned to look at her like the rest of the crowd.

Oh no! What happens if they recognize me? Supergirl thought.

But she could tell by their expressions that they did not know who she was. That gave Supergirl the confidence to walk right past them and into the stadium.

CHAPTER 4

LET THE GAMES BEGIN!

Supergirl stood at one end of the stadium with the rest of the competitors. A complex obstacle course lay before them. Tall towers rose from the ground. Deep pits let out clouds of smoke. Objects that Supergirl could not name floated in the air.

Every seat in the stadium was filled. Supergirl could hear and feel the roar of the excited crowd. Her metal armor shook from the intense sound. And then the cheering doubled when Darkseid arrived.

"DARKSEID! DARKSEID! DARKSEID!" the crowd chanted.

The Dark Lord of Apokolips took his seat in the Royal Box. His body looked as if it had been shaped out of the toughest rock in the universe. His face had a permanent frown. His eyes glowed with crimson fire.

I've seen that guy before, Supergirl thought.

ZAP!

That is getting annoying! Supergirl thought as she shook her head.

When Prince Kalibak took the seat next to his father, Darkseid, Supergirl tried to see the family resemblance. Kalibak's eyes did not glow. But father and son did share the same scowl.

Darkseid held up one hand. The crowd fell silent.

"I have commanded the Cinder Games be held as a test of the warriors of Apokolips," Darkseid said. "The winning warrior will become one of my personal guards."

The competitors on the field cheered.

"The Cinder Games of Apokolips have only one rule," Darkseid announced. "And it is that there are no rules! This is a trial of speed, strength, and skill. Whoever completes the course first, wins!"

The competitors cheered again. The crowd roared. Darkseid fired two powerful Omega Beams from his eyes. The twin rays of energy shot into the sky and exploded like fireworks.

The Cinder Games had begun!

Supergirl raced toward the first obstacle at super-speed. She was ahead of everyone in seconds.

This made Stompa angry. The Female Fury stomped on the ground.

RUMMMBLE! CRAAACK!

Large cracks opened up in the ground. Some of the warriors fell into them. Others jumped aside. Supergirl did not see the crack racing toward her from behind. She fell into the deep pit.

"Ha, ha, ha!" Stompa laughed as she ran past.

But Supergirl did not stay down for long. She leaped out of the pit and raced after her rivals. She caught up to them at the base of a tall, round tower—the first obstacle.

Many of the warriors were already climbing the tower. They used the built-in handholds and footholds to work their way to the top.

That looks too easy, Supergirl thought.
There must be a hidden trick.

Suddenly metal battering rams shot out at random spots on the tower. They smacked into some of the competitors. The warriors went flying. Supergirl zoomed at super-speed and caught them before they hit the ground.

"Fool! You could have gotten rid of some of your competition," one of the rescued warriors said. He shoved Supergirl aside.

"You're welcome," Supergirl muttered.

When Supergirl looked up at the tower, she saw that Lashina and Stompa were almost at the top. Lashina used her whip to swing upward. Stompa simply smashed the battering rams. The other warriors were using the handholds and footholds, trying not to get knocked off.

Hmmm. There's no rule that says I have to climb when I can jump, Supergirl thought. *There are no rules.*

Supergirl used her super-strength to take a mighty leap. The crowd gasped as they watched her land on top of the tower in a single bound. Then they cheered wildly.

SNAAKK!

Suddenly a metal whip wrapped around Supergirl's ankles. Lashina climbed onto the top of the tower and grinned in triumph.

"You got up here fast, but you're going back down even faster," Lashina said.

The Female Fury yanked the whip. But her foe did not fall. Thanks to her super-strength, Supergirl stood as firm as a boulder.

"Or not," Supergirl replied.

Supergirl reached down, broke the whip in two, and stepped free of it. Then she used a puff of freeze breath to form blocks of ice around Lashina's boots.

"Stay here while I go win the Cinder Games," Supergirl said and rushed to the second obstacle.

A string of floating rods spread out before her. It looked like a horizontal rope ladder without the rope. The rods did not stay in one place either. They shifted up, down, and sideways. Supergirl was confident she could run across at super-speed. But as soon as her foot touched the first rod, it spun away.

"Whoops!" Supergirl said in surprise.

Supergirl started to fall, but she reached out. She grabbed the rod, hanging on with one hand.

Not a moment later, Stompa came stomping along. Supergirl had to use her super-strength to keep her grip.

Stompa laughed as she ran across the moving rods. Supergirl did not know how the Female Fury kept her footing, but it did not matter. She had to keep going. Supergirl swung from rod to rod like a kid on a set of monkey bars. She passed below Stompa and got to the next obstacle ahead of her rival.

Supergirl stayed ahead of Stompa and the other warriors as she worked through the obstacle course. She was excited to use her speed, strength, and other skills to the fullest.

The crowd was excited too. They had never seen anyone like this Mysterious Warrior. Her abilities were amazing. Her armor was magnificent. And yet no one knew who she was!

Darkseid wondered if Granny Goodness had been keeping one of her trainees a secret as a surprise. He knew he could find out the warrior's identity, but he decided that he enjoyed the mystery.

At last, Supergirl stood on top of the final obstacle. It was another tower. But Supergirl couldn't see a way down to the ground. There were no handholds or ladders or ropes.

The only way off this thing is to fly, Supergirl thought.

ZAP!

Supergirl shook her head. *I . . . I can't fly. There has to be some hidden solution.*

Behind her, Supergirl could hear Stompa, Lashina, and the other competitors finally catching up. She did not have time to figure out the answer.

Supergirl looked down at the moat of steaming . . . *something* . . . that surrounded the base of tower.

That does not smell pleasant, Supergirl thought. *But I have to go win the Cinder Games.*

So Supergirl jumped off the tower.

CHAPTER 5

A Mysterious Warrior Revealed

Supergirl fell through the air. Something deep, deep inside her urged her to stretch out and soar.

The headband sent out two sharp sparks.

ZAP! ZAP!

Instead, Supergirl twisted like an acrobat. She landed on her feet at the outside edge of the smelly pit. Then she ran toward the finish line.

"*NOOO!*" Stompa yelled as she jumped off the tower.

The Female Fury landed a short distance from Supergirl. The impact created huge cracks in the ground. Some of them hit the base of the tower.

The tower started to tip. The competitors still at the top shouted in alarm.

Supergirl's super-hearing picked up the warriors' cries even over the roar of the crowd. She stopped, turned, and saw the danger. Stompa lumbered past her with a laugh.

I have a choice, Supergirl realized. *If I let the competitors fall, I can beat Stompa. If I rescue them, I could lose my chance at victory.*

Supergirl dashed toward the tower.

I have to use my powers to help those people! Supergirl thought.

Supergirl grabbed the damaged base of the tower. The warriors hung on as she used her super-strength to slowly lower it down on its side. Once it was on the ground, Supergirl's rivals jumped off safely, including Lashina. Then they all rushed past her.

"Fool," Lashina said as she ran.

I'm not beaten yet, Supergirl thought.

Using her super-strength, Supergirl took another mighty leap. She sailed over the heads of her competitors.

THWOMP!

Supergirl landed right in front of the finish line and then calmly walked over it.

The crowd erupted in wild cheers. The rest of the competitors battled for second place.

PING!

The Mother Box chimed. In all the excitement, Supergirl had forgotten it was tucked in her belt. The device whispered in her mind. Its power was failing. Supergirl's armor and car would soon turn back to ruined bits.

Oh no! Granny will recognize me. I can't let her know I came to the Cinder Games without her permission, Supergirl thought. *I have to leave . . . now!*

"I declare a winner of the Cinder Games!" Darkseid said from the Royal Box. "Victorious warrior! Present yourself!"

The competitors looked around for the Mysterious Warrior, but Supergirl had already zoomed out of the stadium at super-speed. When she reached her magnificent car, it was turning to junk. A few seconds later, her armor started to fall apart too.

"Oh no," Supergirl groaned.

She quickly scooped up the pieces of her armor and rushed back to the training center. There, she dumped the metal junk onto a trash heap with a heavy sigh.

"Well, that was exciting while it lasted," Supergirl said to the Mother Box.

PING!

A wave of pride poured out from the device, but it was very weak.

"You used almost all of your power to help me with my dream of competing in the Cinder Games," Supergirl said. "Thank you so much! Is there any way I can help you recharge?"

The thought of needing to rest whispered through her mind.

Supergirl tucked the Mother Box into a pocket in her apron and gave it a gentle pat. A moment later, she heard a familiar shout.

"Girl!"

Supergirl ran into the training center. Granny Goodness had returned with Stompa and Lashina.

"Girl, bring us food!" Granny ordered.

Supergirl raced to the kitchen, but she wanted to know what had happened at the Games after she left. She listened to their conversation with her super-hearing.

"Who was that Mysterious Warrior?" Lashina asked. "I didn't recognize that shining armor."

"No one did. But why would anyone win the Cinder Games and then keep their identity a secret?" Stompa asked.

"It won't be secret for long," Granny said. "Darkseid ordered Kalibak to find the Mysterious Warrior. And he's starting his search at the training center."

When Supergirl heard this, she nearly dropped the tray of food she was carrying. *I'm the Mysterious Warrior! But I have no way to prove it,* she thought. *My armor is wrecked and in the trash heap!*

It was not long before Kalibak arrived with a group of Parademons. Granny Goodness brought all her trainees out onto the practice field for him to check.

Supergirl secretly watched from the trash dump. She held the crushed helmet and wished that it could magically transform back into the wonderful battle helm.

ping . . .

A thought whispered through Supergirl's mind: *Don't be afraid. You have more power than you know.*

"That's right. I have abilities no one else does," Supergirl said to herself. "I don't need armor to prove it."

Supergirl dropped the helmet and marched out onto the practice field.

"Girl! What are you doing! You don't belong here!" Granny Goodness shouted.

"Yes, I do," Supergirl said. "I am the Mysterious Warrior!"

Kalibak looked doubtful. Stompa and Lashina laughed.

Supergirl blasted Lashina's feet with a gust of freeze breath. The Fury was frozen to the ground, just like during the Cinder Games.

Lashina looked shocked. "That was *you!*" she yelled.

Stompa gave a shout and rushed over to ram the Super Hero. Supergirl stood as steady as a pillar of steel. Stompa bounced off Supergirl and fell to the ground.

Granny Goodness was furious. She fired a crackling blast of energy at Supergirl with her mega-rod.

ZAAAT!

Supergirl fell to one knee.

That energy strengthens me, the Mother Box whispered. *Make her fire again.*

Supergirl got up off her knee and stood.

"Defiant girl!" Granny snarled. She fired the mega-rod a second time.

ZAAAT!

PING!

The Mother Box rose up out of Supergirl's apron pocket. It glowed brightly with its new energy boost. Armor parts flew out of the nearby trash heaps and settled onto Supergirl. Then they transformed into her magnificent Cinder Games armor.

"You really are the Mysterious Warrior!" Kalibak gasped.

"More than that," Supergirl said as she took the metal band off her head. "That last blast let the Mother Box destroy your hold over me, Granny Goodness. No more headband zapping."

Supergirl crushed the metal band.

"I remember who I am now," she said. "I'm a Super Hero, a protector, a defender of the planet Earth. I am *Supergirl!*"

"*Hmph.* That's too bad. Trainees, attack!" Granny ordered.

"Halt! Protect the Mysterious Warrior! Darkseid commands it!" Kalibak shouted.

Kalibak's Parademons rushed to protect Supergirl. Granny's trainees did the opposite. But Supergirl flew up into the air out of everyone's reach.

BOOM!

The Mother Box opened a Boom Tube.

"It's time for me to go home and get back to saving the world," Supergirl said as she flew through the portal.

BOOM!

The portal closed. The only thing left behind was a single boot from the magnificent armor.

THE ORIGINAL STORY:
CINDERELLA

Once upon a time, there was a young girl who was as kind as she was beautiful. Her mother died, and soon her father remarried. The stepmother was cruel. Her two daughters were vain and selfish. The stepmother forced the girl to become like a servant, doing all the cooking and cleaning. She had to sleep in the cinders of the fireplace, and her stepsisters gave her the nickname "Cinderella."

One day the prince of the kingdom invited all the young ladies of the land to a grand ball so that he could find a wife. Cinderella's stepsisters were very excited to attend. But even as Cinderella helped them dress, they taunted her and said she was not allowed to go. After they left for the ball, Cinderella wept in despair.

But then Cinderella's godmother appeared. She used a magic spell to transform Cinderella's tattered clothing into a beautiful gown with glass slippers. She turned a pumpkin into a coach, mice into horses, and a rat into a coachman.

Cinderella went to the ball. Her stepmother and stepsisters did not recognize her, and the prince fell in love with her at once. But the godmother's spell ended at midnight. As the clock struck twelve, Cinderella had to leave in a hurry. In her rush, she left behind a single glass slipper.

The prince found the slipper and looked for the girl it fit. He searched the kingdom until he found her—Cinderella!

SUPERPOWERED TWISTS

- Cinderella's stepmother and stepsisters are mean and cruel to her. In this story, Supergirl is bossed around by Granny Goodness and her two Female Furies. As warriors of Apokolips, they are naturally cruel and heartless.

- Cinderella's godmother magically dresses the young girl with a gorgeous gown and gives her a coach. The little Mother Box assembles special armor for Supergirl and creates a fabulous car.

- Instead of attending a ball, Supergirl competes against other warriors in the challenging Cinder Games!

- In the fairy tale, Cinderella wins the heart of the prince but has to rush out of the ball before the godmother's spell ends. In this adventure, Supergirl wins the Games, but needs to zoom away before the Mother Box runs out of power.

- The fairy tale prince searches for the girl who fits the glass slipper. Kalibak searches for the winner of the Games. In both stories, they find who they are looking for. Sadly, Kalibak is left with only a boot!

TALK ABOUT IT

1. This adventure is set on the planet Apokolips. Is this a place you would want to visit? Why or why not? Use examples from the story to explain your answer.

2. Supergirl was disappointed when Granny Goodness stopped her from going to the Cinder Games. Have you ever felt left out? Talk about your experience.

3. During the Games, Supergirl turned back to help the other warriors when they were in danger. What does this choice tell you about her character?

WRITE ABOUT IT

1. Make a list of at least three ways the Mother Box helped Supergirl. Then, write a paragraph about why you think the little device came to the hero's aid.

2. Imagine the memory-blocking headband wasn't destroyed. How would the story have played out differently? Write a new ending!

3. Fairy tales are often told and retold over many generations, and the details can change depending on who tells them. Write your version of the "Cinderella" story. Change a lot or a little, but make it your own!

The Author

Laurie S. Sutton has been reading comics since she was a kid. She grew up to become an editor for Marvel, DC Comics, Starblaze, and Tekno Comics. She has written Adam Strange for DC, Star Trek: Voyager for Marvel, plus Star Trek: Deep Space Nine and Witch Hunter for Malibu Comics. There are long boxes of comics in her closet where there should be clothing and shoes. Laurie has lived all over the world and currently resides in Florida.

The Illustrators

Agnes Garbowska is an artist who has worked with many major book publishers, illustrating such brands as DC Super Hero Girls, Teen Titans Go!, My Little Pony, and Care Bears. She was born in Poland and came to Canada at a young age. Being an only child, she escaped into a world of books, cartoons, and comics. She currently lives in the United States and enjoys sharing her office with her two little dogs.

Sil Brys is a colorist and graphic designer. She has worked on many comics and children's books, having had fun coloring stories for Teen Titans Go!, Scooby-Doo, Tom & Jerry, Looney Tunes, DC Super Hero Girls, Care Bears, and more. She lives in a small village in Argentina, where her home is also her office. She loves to create there, surrounded by forests, mountains, and a lot of books.

armory (AR-muh-ree)—a place where weapons are made or stored

battering ram (BAH-tuh-ring RAM)—a large, heavy object used to knock things down or over

cinder (SIN-dur)—a small piece of burned wood, coal, or other material

competitor (kuhm-PEH-tuh-tuhr)—a person who is trying to win in a sport, game, or other contest

defiant (dih-FY-uhnt)—showing a desire to fight against orders and not do what you are told

obstacle (OB-stuh-kuhl)—something that blocks the path forward

portal (POR-tuhl)—an opening that leads from one place to another

rival (RY-vuhl)—a person trying to get the same thing or achieve the same goal as someone else

trainee (tray-NEE)—someone who is in training and learning to take on a certain job or role

transform (trans-FORM)—to change completely

warrior (WAR-ee-ur)—a person skilled in fighting

READ THEM ALL!

THE AMAZON PRINCESS
AND THE PEA

Sutton • Garbowska • Brys

SUPERGIRL
AND THE CINDER GAMES

Sutton • Garbowska • Brys

LITTLE ROBIN'S
FIGHTING HOOD

Stephens • Garbowska • Brys

BATMAN
AND THE BEANSTALK

Stephens • Garbowska • Brys